my to trip
Washington, D.C.

PELICAN PUBLISHING COMPANY
Gretna 2006

Author: JoAnn Polley
Illustrations: Kevin R. Hanstick
Photos: PhotoDisc™ and Vinings Publishing
Design: Infinite Ideas & Designs Inc.
Copyright © 2006 Vinings Publishing
All rights reserved
ISBN: 978-1-58980-360-2
Printed in China
Published by Pelican Publishing Company, Inc.
1000 Burmaster Street, Gretna, Louisiana 70053

Introduction

*A*re you ready to have a blast in the nation's capital? It has so many adventures, you won't know where to begin and you won't ever want it to end. Not only can you visit the actual home of the president, or go to the top of a 555-foot obelisk, or touch a piece of the moon, but you can also crawl through a replica of an African termites' mound at the O. Orkin Insect Zoo in the National Museum of Natural History! Welcome to Washington, D.C.! Pierre L'Enfant planned this city under the direction of President George Washington. For the past 200 years the city has been growing to what you see today, and continues to grow. Museums, parks, office buildings, and monuments occupy the lovely tree-lined streets. Wherever you walk, you will see something happening. And no matter when you visit, be it spring, summer, fall, or winter, you will find plenty of exciting activities to keep you busy. And that's where this book will come in handy. Use it to record all the awesome sights you see so you will have a neat collection of mementos and memories of your wonderful visit.

my trip to Washington, D.C.

Table of Contents

Table of Contents

The First Day of
my trip

*U*se this page to record all kinds of
important information about your trip.

Dates I am visiting

_____

How I arrived

_____

People with me

_____

Where I am staying

_____

Things I plan on buying

_____

Important things I want to see

_____

Neat places I want to go

_____

Cool restaurants where I want to eat

_____

Fun things that I want to do

_____

my trip *to* Washington, D.C.

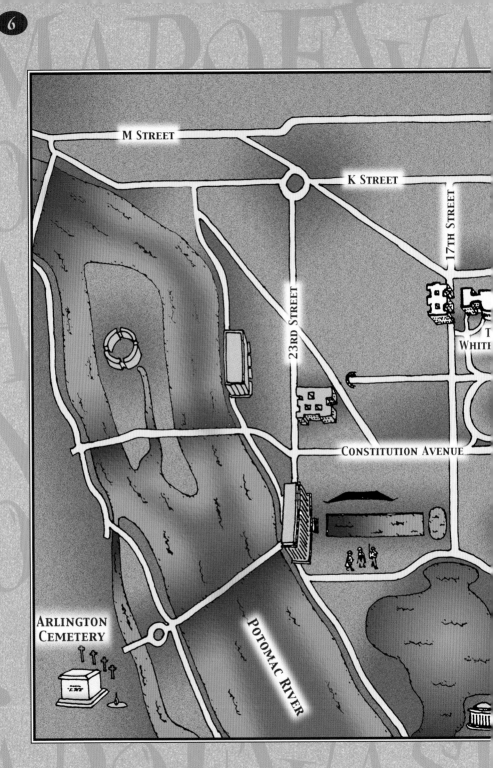

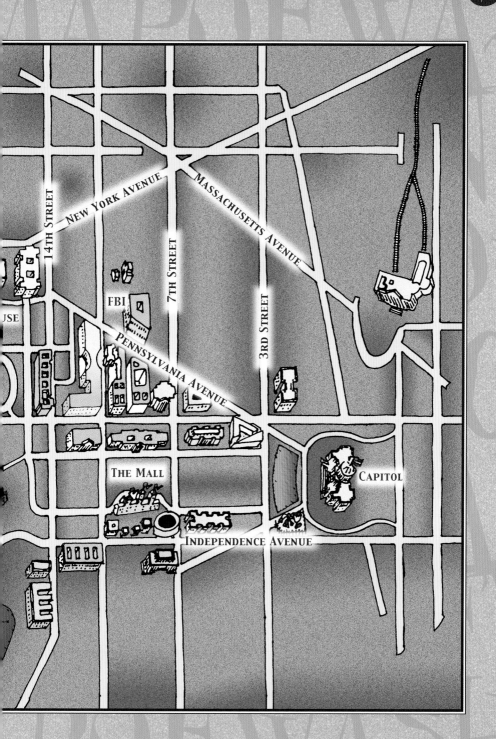

my trip to Washington, D.C.

8

It was with much fanfare on September 18, 1793 that President George Washington, using a marble-headed gavel and a silver trowel, laid a silver plate marking the 13th year of American-independence onto the cornerstone. Curiously enough, that cornerstone has since disappeared and has never been found. But that doesn't detract from this magnificent monument, originally designed by Dr. William Thornton, an amateur architect, with additions and rebuilding done over time by numerous other architects.

THE

THE CAPITOL

Day I visited

_____

The first thing I noticed was

_____

It reminded me of

_____

_____

_____

_____

What really impressed me

_____

_____

_____

_____

_____

_____

I would really like to

_____

_____

_____

my trip to Washington, D.C.

*L*ike to read? Well this library is not only the nation's largest, but it happens to be the largest library in the world. Every book published in the United States must be deposited here for copyright, thus contributing to its enormous size and collection. Although you can't check out any of the books from its more than 500 miles of shelves, you can request to look at any book there. The architecture, based on the Paris Opera House, seems the perfect place to present the impressive Gutenberg Bible and Giant Bible of Mainz, and participate in the noble act of reading.

Library of Congress

Day I visited

_____

The first thing I noticed was

_____

The neatest thing I saw was

_____
_____
_____
_____

The best part about this building was

_____
_____
_____
_____
_____
_____

I would/wouldn't like to come back here because

_____
_____
_____

my trip to Washington, D.C.

SUPREME COURT

Oyez! Oyez! (French legalese for "Hear ye, hear ye.") This gleaming white marble structure of classical Corinthian architecture was designed in 1935 by Cass Gilbert, and is the center where the nine supreme court justices render the last word on every controversial issue facing our nation. If the timing is right, try to hear one of the half-hour sessions held on Mondays at 10 A.M. when the justices release orders and opinions. If you like what you hear, you just may decide on a career in law.

Day I visited

_____

How we got there

_____

Who was with me

_____
_____
_____
_____

Most interesting thing about the court

_____
_____
_____
_____
_____
_____

Fun fact to tell someone at home

_____
_____
_____

my trip to Washington, D.C.

"TO BE OR NOT TO BE"
amazed at this museum.

Well, you will be amazed when you enter the Neoclassical white marble art-deco building designed by architect Paul Phillipe Cret for the 19th–century oil magnate Henry Clay Folger. This world–class library on Shakespeare and the Renaissance is decorated throughout with scenes from the Bard's plays, and the gallery is designed as an Elizabethan Great Hall where you can see various exhibits from the library's extensive collection. And the inn-yard theater even has performances of baroque opera and chamber music to keep you in the Renaissance mood.

Folger Shakespeare Library

Day I visited

_____

The first thing I noticed was

_____

The nicest scene was

_____
_____
_____
_____

The gallery reminded me of

_____
_____
_____
_____
_____

I would/wouldn't like to come back here because

_____
_____
_____

my trip to Washington, D.C.

PRESIDENTIAL WORD SCRAMBLE

ANGERA
◯◯ _ _ _ _

NICNOLL
_ _ _ ◯◯ _ _

MANTUR
_ ◯◯◯ _ _

CRERAT
_ _ _ ◯◯ _

LOPK
◯ _ _ _

SHUB
_ ◯◯ _ _

EVEN THE BEST TENNIS PLAYERS DON'T PLAY HERE.

_ _ _ _ _ _ _ _ _   _ _ _ _ _

All Aboard!

Union Station

This impressive structure designed by architect Daniel H. Burnham features Roman arches, marble fountains, and 36 sculptures of Roman soldiers gazing down from the balcony. The statues, sculpted by Saint-Gaudens were originally nude, as they would have been in Roman times, but the station administrators requested that they be partially covered up so as not to offend anyone. Visit the numerous restaurants and shops as you wander through the cavernous halls.

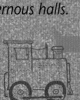

Day I visited

_____

The first thing I noticed was

_____

I thought the neatest statue was

_____

_____

_____

What Union Station looks like

_____

_____

_____

_____

I would/wouldn't like to come back here because

_____

_____

_____

National postal museum

nce Washington's main post office, it opened July 30, 1993 as a museum devoted to the history of the U.S. Postal Service. The 90-foot central hall teems with historic mail planes and antique vehicles such as an 1850s stagecoach. The museum also features interactive exhibits such as a train robbery video, and recreation of early postal routes. Look in the stamp display to see if you can find the stamp that was issued the year you were born.

Day I visited

_____

The first thing I noticed was

_____

The museum is made of

_____

_____

_____

_____

What the stamp from my birth year looks like

_____

_____

_____

_____

_____

_____

I would/wouldn't like to come back here because

_____

_____

Washington, D.C.

Anacostia
Museum
FOR AFRICAN-AMERICAN HISTORY AND CULTURE

This Smithsonian facility will introduce you to the African-American culture with its diverse exhibits of art and history. Founded in 1967 as an experimental program for Washington's black community, this facility grew into a museum dedicated to increasing public understanding and knowledge of the African-American experience. Outside you can take a guided walk along the George Washington Carver nature trail.

Day I visited

The first thing I noticed was

My favorite exhibit was

The Carver nature trail looks like

I would/wouldn't like to come back here because

my trip to Washington, D.C.

Frederick Douglass National Historic Site

This historic site was home to Frederick Douglass from 1878 until his death in 1895. Douglass, born into poverty and slavery, rose to become a leading abolitionist, orator and publisher during the Civil War. As a spokesman for the downtrodden, he commanded tremendous respect and over the years acquired numerous gifts from such notable people as Queen Victoria, and Mary Todd Lincoln, which are on display in this museum.

Day I visited

What I thought was cool

What really interested me

What I liked the most

I would/wouldn't like to come back here because

my trip to Washington, D.C.

STAMPS AND POSTCARDS

Don't forget to write
your friends and family back home.

Names	Addresses

my trip to Washington, D.C.

Brochures

Collect brochures from all the interesting places you visit:

Albert Einstein Planetarium
National Zoological Park
Anacostia Museum
National Air and Space Museum
Smithsonian Castle
Ford's Theatre and Museum
National Aquarium
Textile Museum
Department of the Treasury
International Spy Museum
National Museum of American Art
U.S. Botanic Garden
Georgetown
Washington Monument

my trip to Washington, D.C.

Are you into espionage? Then this is the museum for you. Prepare to enter the shadowy world of the secret agent as you visit The International Spy Museum. On exhibit are more than 200 gadgets, weapons and technologies used by spies over the years. As you visit the various galleries you can learn all about microdots, surveillance equipment and numerous devices such as a poison umbrella that was actually used to deliver a fatal dose!

International Spy Museum

Day I visited

_____

What I thought was cool

_____

What really interested me

_____
_____
_____
_____
_____

What I would remember

_____
_____
_____
_____
_____
_____
_____

I would/wouldn't like to come back here because

_____
_____
_____

my trip to Washington, D.C.

U.S. Botanic Garden

Take time to smell the flowers. And you'll have plenty of opportunity here on six acres of lush landscaping which offer over 8,000 tropical and subtropical plants that surround small reflecting pools and ponds. You can thank John Quincy Adams, Benjamin Latrobe and a host of other distinguished Washingtonians for this earthly paradise. In 1816, they founded the Colombian Institute for the promotion of arts and sciences, in which a branch of the Institute, the Washington Botanical Society documented the local flora and fauna, and from this evolved the very garden in which you are standing.

Day I visited

How I felt

What I liked best

My favorite flower looks like

I would/wouldn't like to come back here because

my trip to Washington, D.C.

Imagine if you will, the Union's greatest general, who went on to become our 18th President, astride his horse at the Vicksburg Campaign, leading his troops toward one of the most decisive victories of the Civil War. This monumental equestrian structure, designed jointly by sculptor Henry Merwin Shrady and architect Edward Pearce Casey, took over 20 years to complete, and stands 252–feet long, and 70–feet wide.

Ulysses S. Grant Memorial

Day I visited

_____

The first thing I noticed was

_____

The best part of the sculpture was

_____
_____
_____
_____

What I would tell my friends about this sculpture

_____
_____
_____
_____
_____
_____
_____

I would/wouldn't like to come back here because

_____
_____
_____

my trip to Washington, D.C.

The Mall

This is the heart of Washington, DC, created over 200 years ago by Pierre L'Enfant who made this beautiful sweep of lawn the city's centerpiece. Bordered on both sides by some of the world's most famous museums, monuments, gardens and sculptures, you can spend hours entertaining yourself in this one area. If the weather is right, take a ride on the 1940s carousel designed by Allan Herschell, which has 58 horses, two chariots, and a sea dragon.

Day I visited

_____

What the best part was

_____

My description of the carousel

_____
_____
_____
_____

What I'd like more time to see

_____
_____
_____
_____
_____
_____

My favorite sculpture was

_____
_____

my trip to Washington, D.C.

Get ready for an incredible artistic experience. The East Gallery, a trapezoidal structure considered one of the country's ten best buildings, is where you can feast your eyes on a three-story high Calder mobile and a vibrant Miro tapestry. As you wander around the gallery, look for a particular work of art that really impresses you. Think about it for awhile, and then write down your feelings about what caught your attention and why this piece of art made an impression.

National Gallery of Art

EAST GALLERY

Day I visited

_____

The first thing I noticed was

_____

The Miro tapestry is made of

_____

_____

_____

_____

My favorite piece of art was

_____

_____

_____

_____

_____

_____

I would/wouldn't like to come back here because

_____

_____

my trip to Washington, D.C.

The incredible artistic experience continues in the West Gallery, where you can take in over 5,000 European and American paintings and sculptures dating from the 13th– to the 19th–centuries, including DaVinci, Botticelli and Whistler. Look at the changes in subject matter and style as the centuries pass. Find a painting or sculpture that really impresses you and then see if you can find others of the same style. Then, write about the similarities between the works, and why you liked them the best.

National Gallery of Art
WEST GALLERY

Day I visited

_____

The first thing I noticed was

_____

The art that most impressed me was

_____
_____
_____
_____
_____

The style that I liked the most and why

_____
_____
_____
_____
_____
_____

I would/wouldn't like to come back here because

_____
_____
_____

my trip
to
Washington, D.C.

Be sure to visit the world–famous sculpture garden where you can sit on the benches or lie on the grass as you contemplate the works around you.

SCULPTURE
GARDEN
ON THE MALL

Day I visited

_____

The first thing I noticed was

_____

What the sculptures are made of

_____
_____
_____
_____

What the benches look like

_____
_____
_____
_____
_____
_____

I would/wouldn't like to come back here because

_____
_____
_____

my trip to Washington, D.C.

It's said that diamonds are a girl's best friend and now you can see the famous Hope Diamond, a 45-carat stone once owned by Louis XIV, and considered to be one of the most perfect diamonds in the world. But if your taste runs to the more earthly offers, look around for the more than 300 birds exhibited, or visit the O. Orkin Insect Zoo where you can inspect tarantulas, cockroaches, bees, ants and millipedes to your heart's content.

National Museum Of Natural History

Day I visited

_____

Who I'd like to tell this about

_____

What a diamond is made of

_____

_____

_____

_____

What my favorite bird looks like

_____

_____

_____

_____

_____

_____

I would/wouldn't like to come back here because

_____

_____

my trip to Washington, D.C.

Draw A DINOSAUR

my trip to Washington, D.C.

Oh, say can you see...

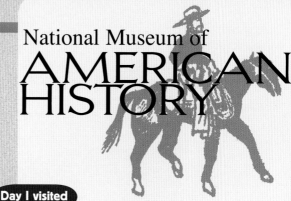

National Museum of AMERICAN HISTORY

The original Star-Spangled Banner that inspired our national anthem is housed in this museum, along with three floors of exhibits that cover over 200 years of our country's history. Be sure to test your skills in the Hands-On History Room where you can try to ride a high-wheeler bike, use Eli Whitney's cotton gin and look into the life of a mid-1800s immigrant. End your tour with a visit to a turn-of-the century ice cream parlor complete with etched-glass mirrors, potted palms and wicker.

Day I visited

_____

The first thing I noticed was

_____

What I liked the best

_____
_____
_____

What I'll tell my friends

_____
_____
_____
_____
_____

I would/wouldn't like to come back here because

_____
_____

my trip to Washington, D.C.

Opened just in time for the United States Bicentennial on July 1, 1976, this huge pinkish marble monolithic museum will keep you flying high! Don't be embarrassed to lay down on the floor under the planes suspended from the ceiling to get the full impact of them in flight. Be sure to check out "To Fly" on the 5–story IMAX screen for a flight you'll never forget!

National Air and Space

Museum

Day I visited

_____

The first thing I noticed was

_____

The planes are made of

_____

_____

_____

_____

_____

I thought the movie was

_____

_____

_____

_____

_____

I would/wouldn't like to come back here because

_____

_____

my trip to Washington, D.C.

Hirshhorn
MUSEUM

If sculpture is your thing, pay close attention to the magnificent works by Rodin, Matisse, Calder, and other famous pieces, which were donated by Joseph Hirshhorn from his private collection. Opened in 1974, this museum of contemporary art has become the fifth most–visited museum in the United States due to its outstanding collection.

Day I visited

The first thing I noticed was

The current exhibit was

What my favorite sculpture looked like

I would/wouldn't like to come back here because

RDPII-142

my trip to Washington, D.C.

National Museum
of
African Art

he only museum in the United States completely dedicated to the presentation of African Art celebrates the diverse culture with a fascinating collection of wood, fiber, cloth, and ivory artifacts. Many of the pieces were used in day-to-day life, rituals and ceremonies, and provide an excellent educational insight into the African community.

Day I visited

_____

The first thing I noticed was

_____

African Art is made of

_____
_____
_____
_____

Countries in Africa whose art I saw

_____
_____
_____
_____
_____

I would/wouldn't like to come back here because

_____
_____
_____

my trip to Washington, D.C.

Smithsonian Castle

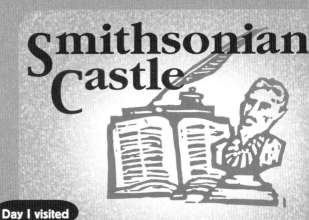

This internationally renowned gothic style institution houses millions of catalogued pieces of art in its vast complex. It all started in 1826 with a gift of around $500,000 from a British scientist named James Smithson who wanted to establish an institution "for the increase and diffusion of knowledge among men." The increase in knowledge that has arisen from his generosity has infinitely exceeded his initial contribution.

Day I visited

_____

The first thing I noticed was

_____

The building reminded me of

_____

_____

_____

I was most impressed by

_____

_____

_____

_____

_____

I would/wouldn't like to come back here because

_____

_____

RDPII-142   3

my trip *to* Washington, D.C.

Arts and Industries Building

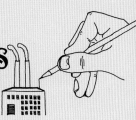

Designed by Adolph Cluss in 1880 and completed in 1881 just in time for James Garfield's Inaugural Ball, this building is the second oldest Smithsonian Museum on the mall. It was the first building in the city to have electric lights and movable walls, which came in handy since the building was originally designed to exhibit objects from Philadelphia's 1876 Centennial Exposition. In fact, the east and west halls still contain some of the items from the exposition, including Lincoln's autopsy kit.

Day I visited

_____

The first thing I noticed was

_____

My favorite thing from the fair was

_____
_____
_____
_____

The 1876 expo shows me that

_____
_____
_____
_____
_____
_____

I would/wouldn't like to come back here because

_____
_____
_____

my trip to Washington, D.C.

Freer Gallery of Art/ Arthur M. Sackler Gallery

Into Asian art? Well, you won't be disappointed if you visit these amazing galleries. Arthur M. Sackler, a medical researcher dedicated to extensive learning, donated the Sackler's pieces, over 1,000 of them spanning over 5,000 years of time. And the Freer Gallery, named for Detroit industrialist Charles Lang Freer, has a fabulous collection that spans 6,000 years! In addition, be sure to see the Freer collection of over 1,200 Whistler pieces—you won't be disappointed.

Day I visited

Who was with me

My favorite piece of art was

I liked/disliked Japanese screens because

Oriental art seems different from other art because

my trip to Washington, D.C.

NATIONAL MUSEUM OF
WOMEN IN THE ARTS

National Museum of
Women in the Arts

Once a men's only Masonic Temple, this lovely 1907 Renaissance Revival building now offers over 1,200 paintings, prints, and sculpture by prominent women artists such as Georgia O'Keefe, Mary Cassatt, and Frida Kahlo. This collection spans five centuries of artistic work, thus demonstrating women's contribution to the artistic community. As you look at the pieces, try to see if you can relate to what the artist was trying to convey, and note which piece you like the best and why.

Day I visited

_____

The first thing I noticed was

_____

My favorite piece of art was

_____
_____
_____
_____
_____

I lked this artist the best because

_____
_____
_____
_____
_____
_____

I would/wouldn't like to come back here because

_____
_____

my trip to Washington, D.C.

*S*ic semper tyrannis! John Wilkes Booth uttered those words on April 14, 1865, as he fatally wounded President Abraham Lincoln here, thus forever altering the course of American history. Here you can see the clothes Lincoln was wearing when he was shot, as well as Booth's diary and the Derringer he used to assassinate Lincoln. Across the street you can visit the Petersen House, where Lincoln was taken after he was wounded. There the clock is stopped at 7:22 A.M., the time of Lincoln's death the next morning.

Ford's Theatre
AND MUSEUM

Day I visited

_____

The first thing I saw was

_____

The theater seemed

_____
_____
_____
_____

Most interesting thing about the museum

_____
_____
_____
_____
_____
_____

I would/wouldn't like to come back here because

_____
_____

FORD'S THEATRE

MATINEE TODAY
MUSEUM OPEN

my trip to Washington, D.C.

TOP SECRET

FBI Building

This concrete fortress houses our nation's top notch Federal Investigators. As you take the tour, be on the lookout for the Ten Most Wanted, a list that was begun in 1950. See if you recognize anyone on it. Also take note of the vast collection of confiscated weapons in which there are no two exactly alike, even though there are over 5,000 firearms! Finally, get ready for the grand finale with a demonstration of various guns in the firing range. (Tours are scheduled to begin again in the spring of 2007).

Day I visited
_____

The first thing I noticed was
_____

I would/would not like to work for the FBI because
_____
_____
_____
_____
_____

The gun demonstration was/was not cool because
_____
_____
_____
_____
_____
_____

I would/wouldn't like to come back here because
_____
_____
_____

WANTED

my trip to Washington, D.C.

When this post office was completed back in 1899 it was the largest government building in the district, and the first with a clock tower and electric power plant. Try to make it to the top of the 315-foot tower where you can take a look inside the bell ringing chambers, and check out the ten Congress Bells that are rung on national holidays, inaugurations, and the opening and closing of Congress.

OLD
Post Office
TOWER

Day I visited

_____

The first thing I noticed was

_____

The building looked really

_____
_____
_____
_____

The coolest thing about the bell chamber was

_____
_____
_____
_____
_____
_____

I would/wouldn't tell my friends to come here because

_____
_____
_____

my trip to Washington, D.C.

National Archives

John Russell Pope, architect of the National Gallery and Thomas Jefferson Memorial really went all out with this building. There are 72 Corinthian columns that are each 53 feet high, 5 feet 8 inches in diameter, and weigh 95-tons. Inside the rotunda of this building, the original Declaration of Independence, Constitution, and Bill of Rights are on public display. In addition, the Archives holds billions of other important historical documents. To learn more about it, visit www.archives.gov.

Day I visited

_____

The first thing I noticed was

_____

The building reminds me of

_____
_____
_____
_____

Getting to see the Declaration of Independence was

_____
_____
_____
_____
_____
_____

The best part of this visit was

_____
_____
_____

my trip to Washington, D.C.

If you like to do more than just eat fish, take a look at the over 1,700 species located in these tanks. The oldest public aquarium in the nation, this collection has assorted fresh and salt-water fish, as well as eels, alligators, sharks and Japanese carp. Be sure to go over to the touch tank, where you can actually experience a close encounter with various sea life. And be sure to check out the 2 P.M. feeding of either the piranhas or sharks. You'll learn the real meaning of the words "feeding frenzy."

National Aquarium

Day I visited

_____

The first thing I noticed was

_____

My favorite part of the exhibit was

_____

_____

_____

_____

I would/wouldn't like to learn to scuba dive because

_____

_____

_____

_____

_____

_____

The one thing that I will always remember is

_____

_____

my trip to Washington, D.C.

B'nai B'rith Klutznick

National Jewish Museum

As one of the oldest cultures in the world, the Jewish people have quite a history. And here you can see more than 20 centuries of traditional art and ceremonial objects in this amazing collection of religious books, Torahs, and Judaic art, all giving testimonial to the interesting, and extensive life of the Jewish people. Make sure you treat yourself to a stroll through the marvelous sculpture garden.

Day I visited

_____

The first thing I noticed was

_____

The most interesting piece I saw was

_____
_____
_____
_____

My favorite sculpture was

_____
_____
_____
_____
_____

The one thing I would tell my friends about is

_____
_____
_____

my trip to Washington, D.C.

Mad Lib ™

Before looking at the story below, write in what ever words come to mind-in the columns below. Then, fill in the blank spaces with the words-you have picked according to number.

1. Adjective _____
2. Noun _____
3. Adjective _____
4. Person's name _____
5. Place _____
6. Noun _____
7. Noun _____
8. Adjective _____
9. Noun _____
10. Exclamation _____
11. Adverb _____
12. Verb ending in "ing" _____

13. Noun _____
14. Adjective _____
15. Adjective _____
16. Adjective _____
17. Verb _____
18. Noun _____
19. Verb ending in "ing" _____
20. Exclamation _____
21. 1st person's name _____
22. Adverb _____
23. Adjective _____
24. Noun _____

Dear Diary,

Today I got up feeling pretty 1._____. After I ate a/an 2._____

_____, I felt 3._____. I went with 4._____

____ to 5._____. We decided it would be fun to visit a/an 6._____

_____, so we hopped on a/an 7._____ and went down the road

until we came to a/an 8._____ 9._____. 10."_____

_____!" I said, 11._____ as I went 12._____

across the 13._____. "I have never seen such 14._____ monuments in

my life."

I wonder if there are any 15._____ and 16._____

monuments here too?" Let's 17._____ the guidebook to see if we can find a

18._____. Then we can spend the rest of the day 19._____

_____. 20."_____!" 21._____ said, 22._____

_____. Traveling with you is like traveling with a/an 23._____

24._____.

Renwick Gallery

Designed in 1859 specifically to house the private art collection of banker William Wilson Corcoran, these precious pieces were later moved to the Corcoran Gallery and now this building displays a wonderful collection of 20th–century American crafts. But the building retains its 19th–century flavor as the Grand Salon looks exactly as it did for Corcoran's all night balls! Imagine yourself in your finest evening attire, whirling around this exquisite room until the early hours of the morning.

Day I visited

_____

The first thing I noticed was

_____

The best part of the collection was

_____
_____
_____
_____

The Victorian Grand Salon looks like

_____
_____
_____
_____
_____

What I purchased from the Gift Shop

_____
_____

my trip to Washington, D.C.

42

George Hewitt Myers really loved his carpets! And you can see why when you check out the extraordinary rotating collection of over 12,000 carpets and textiles. It all began when George made a simple purchase of a rug for his Yale dormitory room and ended up with what you see today. You really will feel as if you've been on a magic carpet ride once you're finished here.

Textile
M u s e u m

Day I visited

The first thing I noticed was

My favorite textiles were

What I learned about different fibers

I would/wouldn't like to come back here because

my trip to Washington, D.C.

Department of the Treasury

T he oldest of the government's departmental buildings, this structure with its white Ionic colonnade conveys the impression of an ancient Greek temple. Ionic is one of the five classical orders of architecture and its columns have scroll-like ornamentation at the top. Using the ancient classical order is very popular with monuments. See how many other buildings have this type of architecture.

Day I visited

_____

The first thing I noticed was

_____

What they do here

_____
_____
_____
_____

How many columns are on this building

_____
_____
_____
_____
_____

I would/wouldn't like to come back here because

_____
_____

my trip to Washington, D.C.

The WHITE House

E ven though this enormous house, whose construction began in 1792, has seen numerous rebuilding and renovations, there were no closets in it until 1952! Try to visit the East Room, originally designed by the architect James Hoban, as the residence's "public audience room." Here, First Lady Abigail Adams used to dry her laundry. While you're in the room, take a close look at the full length portrait by Gilbert Stuart of George Washington. This is the only object left from when the room was finished in 1800. It survived because Dolley Madison risked capture by waiting to have it removed as the British troops advanced to burn the capital in 1814.

Day I visited

_____

The first thing I noticed was

_____

Did I see Secret Service Agents?

_____

_____

_____

_____

Where the president was the day I was there

_____

_____

_____

_____

_____

_____

I would/wouldn't like to come back here because

_____

_____

_____

_____

my trip to Washington, D.C.

DWIGHT D. EISENHOWER
Executive Office Building

35   36 ▷ 35A

Alfred B. Mullett patterned this building after the Louvre, with 900 freestanding columns, 566 rooms, 18-foot ceilings, and tall chimneys, when it was built between 1871 and 1888. Originally it housed the War, Navy and State departments, but now its spacious offices house various members of the executive branch. Look upward to the spectacular stained glass rotundas and skylit-domes for a spectacular view.

Day I visited

_____

The first thing I noticed was

_____

How close is this building to the White House?

_____
_____
_____
_____
_____

Would I like to work here?

_____
_____
_____
_____
_____
_____

I would/wouldn't like to come back here because

_____
_____

my trip to Washington, D.C.

Look up!

A t 555'-5 1/8", this monument is not only the tallest building in the city, but the tallest freestanding masonry stone structure in the-world! When the monument opened to the public on October 9, 1888, a steam elevator took twelve minutes to carry passengers to the top. The first year it was open, 69,887 people rode the elevator, while 51,984 chose to walk up the 898 steps! Today the modern elevator will take you up quickly, but get ready to take a hike if you are able to take the steps to the bottom, because once you've started down, you can't change your mind.

Washington Monument

Day I visited

Who was with me

What I thought

From the top I could see

my trip to Washington, D.C.

Vietnam Veterans

A competition for the design of this memorial received 1,421 entries. Maya Ying Lin, a 21-year-old undergraduate student at Yale won the competition and you can see her vision reflected in its 140 panels of polished black granite that stretch almost 500 feet, honoring the 58,229 men and women who died or are missing from the war. The names are listed in chronological order, from the first casualty in 1959 until the last one in 1975.

Vietnam Veterans
MEMORIAL

Day I visited
_____

The first thing I noticed was
_____

What I felt when I first started walking through it
_____
_____
_____
_____

I liked/didn't like this memorial because
_____
_____
_____
_____
_____
_____

I would/wouldn't like to come back here because
_____
_____
_____

my trip to Washington, D.C.

48

Lincoln Memorial

Guess what? He's not just on the pennies in your pocket! This great sculpture of the 16th U.S. president, Abraham Lincoln, was designed by Daniel French. It took 28 blocks of marble and 4-years of carving to complete. The huge doric columns (36 of them) represent the number of states in the union at the time of Lincoln's death. The text you see carved into the limestone wall is his Gettysburg Address and Second Inaugural Address.

Day I visited

_____

The first thing I noticed was

_____

What seemed really cool

_____
_____
_____
_____

I really admire Abraham Lincoln because

_____
_____
_____
_____
_____
_____

I would/wouldn't like to come back here because

_____
_____

my trip to Washington, D.C.

Dedicated on July 27, 1995, this memorial depicts 19 stainless-steel statues of poncho-draped soldiers on patrol. The faces on the wall were taken from actual photos of Korean War veterans. By looking at them and their reflections in the black granite wall, you can see 38 figures, thus commemorating the 38th parallel that separates the two Koreas.

Korean War
Veterans
Memorial

Day I visited
_____

The first thing I noticed was
_____

The expressions on their faces seemed
_____
_____
_____
_____
_____

The best part of the memorial was
_____
_____
_____
_____
_____
_____

As I looked at the statues I felt
_____
_____

my trip to Washington, D.C.

Word Search

```
Y  D  E  N  N  E  K  R  E  T  R  A  C
A  F  L  W  X  T  M  S  M  A  D  A  W
C  J  O  H  N  S  O  N  B  K  P  J  L
T  L  M  I  W (S  E  N  A  T  E) H  O
A  N  O  T  G  N  I  H  S  A  W  M  O
L  R  S  E  J  A  X  B  S  Q  H  P  Z
P  S  B  H  N  R  Z  M  Y  T  S  B  L
T  R  U  O  C  E  M  E  R  P  U  S  A
I  M  N  U  R  T  C  D  O  G  B  J  N
D  B  O  S  B  E  P  L  W  T  X  M  O
A  K  G  E  K  V  T  Q  I  A  B  F  I
L  M  A  B  O  M  R  U  P  N  Z  L  T
B  R  T  K  F  A  H  E  M  J  T  N  A
A  U  N  I  O  N  S  T  A  T  I  O  N
S  V  E  B  W  T  C  J  L  G  K  X  N
I  Y  P  F  Z  E  F  Q  L  P  A  I  Y
N  L  O  C  N  I  L  E  B  A  M  N  B
D  R  A  Y  Y  V  A  N  R  D  R  O  F
```

Word List:

Washington	Navy Yard	Lincoln	Nixon
White House	Union Station	Pentagon	Ford
Supreme Court	National Zoo	Clinton	Carter
Embassy Row	FBI	Adams	
Arboretum	Kennedy	Bush	
Vietnam Veteran	Tidal Basin	Reagan	
	Senate	Johnson	

my trip to Washington, D.C.

Thomas Jefferson Memorial

This tribute is to Thomas Jefferson, our third president, one of our nation's founding fathers and author of the Declaration of Independence. Inside the memorial are bronzed inscriptions taken from the Declaration of Independence, including one of the most famous, "We hold these truths to be self-evident, that all men are created equal, that they are endowed by their Creator with certain unalienable rights, that among these are Life, Liberty, and the pursuit of Happiness."

Day I visited

_____

The first thing I noticed was

_____

The monument looked like

_____
_____
_____
_____

This memorial impressed me because

_____
_____
_____
_____
_____
_____

I would/wouldn't like to come back here because

_____
_____

my trip to Washington, D.C.

Although Congress authorized the building of this memorial in 1955, it took until 1991 for the groundbreaking, and until May of 1997 for the dedication. But as you can see from its impressive size, granite walls, fountains and sculptures, it was well worth the wait. And the statue of Eleanor Roosevelt makes her the first First Lady to be honored in a presidential memorial.

FDR Memorial

Day I visited

_____

The first thing I noticed was

_____

I enjoyed the fountains because

_____
_____
_____
_____

I thought the statues were interesting because

_____
_____
_____
_____
_____
_____

I would/wouldn't like to come back here because

_____
_____
_____

my trip to Washington, D.C.

U.S. Holocaust
Memorial Museum

Completed in 1993, and designed by architect James Ingo Freed, a German refugee, this somber riveting memorial dedicated to the millions of Jews, Gypsies, homosexuals and others who were persecuted under the Nazi rule from 1933 to 1945, is bound to elicit powerful emotions. Expect to be moved by the presentation of the horror and tragedy that befell so many. Record your feelings and reactions as you view this testimonial to one of the world's most tragic events.

Day I visited

_____

The first thing I noticed was

_____

What amazed me the most was

_____
_____
_____
_____

This memorial moved me because

_____
_____
_____
_____
_____
_____

I would/wouldn't like to come back here because

_____
_____
_____

my trip to Washington, D.C.

Money, money, everywhere.

This is the place where all your hard-earned cash has been printed since 1914. Although money is printed around the clock, so it would seem like they would have a few dollars to spare, there are no free samples. The process used to print these bills is called "Intaglio". Each sheet picks up its color from lines which are filled with ink that are engraved in heavy steel plates. First the backs are printed, and the faces the next day. And you end with a crisp new bill!

Bureau of Engraving and Printing

Day I visited

_____

The first thing I noticed was

_____

I never knew that

_____
_____
_____
_____

I wish they gave out samples for . . .

_____
_____
_____
_____
_____

I would/wouldn't like to come back here because

_____
_____

my trip to Washington, D.C.

TORPEDO Factory

riginally built to manufacture MK-14 torpedoes and shell cases during World War I and World War II, this building now serves as a studio to over 160 professional artists who work in a variety of media while they create their works before your eyes, allowing you to ask and learn about the various forms of art. And do not miss a visit to the city's Archaeology Museum and Research Lab on the third floor where you can interact with actual archaeologists and learn first hand as they process the artifacts.

Day I visited

_____

The first thing I noticed was

_____

My favorite piece of art was

_____
_____
_____
_____

The kind of artist I'd most like to be is _____ because

_____
_____
_____
_____
_____
_____

The neatest archaeological artifact was

_____
_____
_____

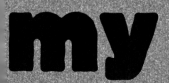 

my trip to Washington, D.C.

First Ladies

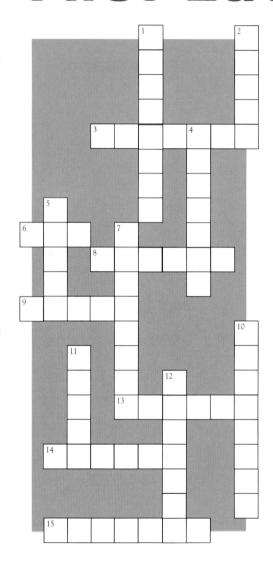

Across

3. Became Senator of NY
6. Had a dog named "Checkers"
8. Went on to marry "Ari"
9. Her last name is a common automobile
13. Married to James Madison
14. Our nation's first first lady
15. Married to #41

Down

1. Married to former peanut farmer
2. Married to Ronnie, former movie star
4. Look on page 44
7. Not Ladybug, but _____
10. Abe's wife
11. Wife of #43
12. FDR's wife

my trip to Washington, D.C.

corcoran gallery
OF ART

Housed inside an 1897 Georgian marble building designed by Ernest Flagg, Washington's oldest private museum of more than 11,000 works has a wonderful collection of 19th–century American art as well as 17th–century Dutch and 19th–century French pieces. In this diverse collection you'll see a variety of styles, and subject matter ranging from lush landscapes to stately portraits. As you gaze upon all the artistic genius, take a while to contemplate the various styles you see. Write a little about which artist and style you seem to like best and why.

Day I visited

_____

The first thing I noticed was

_____

The type of art I liked the most was

_____
_____
_____
_____

The style I liked the least was

_____
_____
_____
_____
_____

I would/wouldn't like to come back here because

_____
_____
_____

my trip to Washington, D.C.

In October 1863, Henry Dunant, a Swiss businessman, founded the International Red Cross movement. The founding of the American Red Cross, which occurred in 1881 as a result of the dedication and devotion of Clara Barton, goes beyond the International Red Cross in that it also covers disasters, such as hurricanes, earthquakes, and tornadoes.

AMERICAN
Red Cross
Museum

Day I visited

_____

What pictures I took

_____

What I discovered

_____
_____
_____
_____

Where I'd like to go next

_____
_____
_____
_____
_____

Where we'll probably go to next

_____
_____

my trip to Washington, D.C.

National **Arboretum**

Established in 1927 for plant and tree research, this 444-acre site will dazzle your senses with its lush collection of old fashioned roses, the nation's finest azaleas, boxwood, daylilies, daffodils and odiferous herbs. For a real treat be certain to visit the magnificent Bonsai collection in the carefully crafted miniatures.

Day I visited

_____

The first thing I noticed was

_____

What was blooming when I was there

_____
_____
_____
_____
_____

What I would most like to take home

_____
_____
_____
_____
_____
_____

I would/wouldn't like to come back here because

_____
_____

my trip to **Washington, D.C.**

DAR Museum

Founded in 1890 by four women who were excluded from a Sons of the American Revolution conference, this organization today consists of several hundred thousand women who are descendants of soldiers who fought in the Revolution. Once inside, you will be in a building that is one of the largest buildings ever built for and owned by women. While you are there, go to the third floor and take a look at the 18th and 19th century children's furniture, toys and dolls.

Day I visited

_____

What DAR stands for

_____

What I checked out on the 3rd floor

_____
_____
_____
_____

Do you have relatives who fought in the Revolution?

_____
_____
_____
_____
_____
_____
_____

I would/wouldn't like to come back here because

_____
_____
_____

my trip to Washington, D.C.

Hains Point

Be sure to visit visit Hains Point, a popular spot for bikers, runners and triathletes in training. There you can see an amazing sculpture entitled "Awakening" by J. Seward Johnson, Jr.. This aluminum giant will take your breath away as you inspect and imagine it attempting to struggle its way out of the earth. What parts of the body do you see, and how do they affect you? What do you think it means?

Day I visited

_____

The first thing I noticed was

_____

I would/wouldn't like to be a sculptor because

_____
_____
_____
_____

What I'll remember most about this site

_____
_____
_____
_____
_____
_____

I would/wouldn't like to come back here because

_____
_____

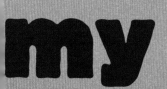

my trip to Washington, D.C.

*L*ook, up in the sky! Is it a bird? Is it a plane? No, it's the Zeiss VI planetarium projector, a bicentennial gift from the people of West Germany, which can re-create almost every celestial phenomenon that is visible to the naked eye. The Albert Einstein Planetarium allows you to embark on an astronomical adventure that you'll never forget as you immerse yourself in a galaxy of about 9,000 stars.

Albert Einstein
Planetarium

Day I visited

_____

The first thing I noticed was

_____

The best part of the exhibit was

_____
_____
_____
_____

I learned that

_____
_____
_____
_____
_____

I would/wouldn't like to come back here because

_____
_____
_____

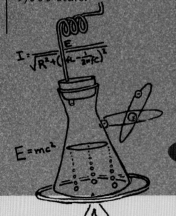

$$I = \frac{E}{\sqrt{R^2 + \left(\omega_L - \frac{1}{2\pi fc}\right)^2}}$$

$$E = mc^2$$

my trip to Washington, D.C.

The John F. Kennedy Center for the
Performing Arts

*I*nto the cultural arts? This fabulous performing arts center built from 1966-1971 on the banks of the Potomac, sports 3,700 tons of Italian Carrera marble on the outside, and the inside houses a 630–foot long room, making it longer than the Washington Monument! Look at the furnishings inside for a real international flavor, as the chandeliers were donated by Sweden, and the tapestries came from France! With five theaters inside offering everything from puppet shows, story telling, opera, and dance, it should be easy to find something that will satisfy your cultural desires.

Day I visited

_____

The first thing I noticed was

_____

What I liked best was

_____

_____

_____

_____

While visiting I got to see

_____

_____

_____

_____

_____

_____

_____

I'm going to tell my friends about

_____

_____

_____

_____

my trip to **Washington, D.C.**

The
U.S. Marine Corps
War Memorial

You are looking at a representation of the 5th Marine Division's capture of Japan's Mount Surabachi on February 23, 1945. Based upon a Pulitzer Prize winning photograph, sculptor Felix de Weldon in 1954 managed to capture that decisive moment in history and memorialize it in this amazing work of art.

Day I visited

_____

The first thing I noticed was

_____

It reminded me of

_____

_____

_____

_____

The sculpture made me feel

_____

_____

_____

_____

_____

I would/wouldn't like to come back here because

_____

_____

my trip to Washington, D.C.

MAPS

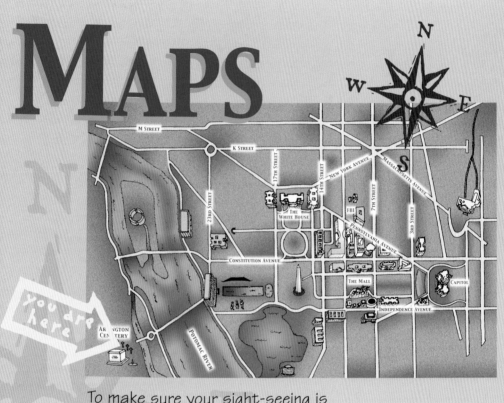

To make sure your sight-seeing is complete, check out the full-size detailed map of the Washington, D.C. area on pages 6–7.

my trip to Washington, D.C.

Ticket Stubs and Souvenirs

Start a scrap book with all the ticket stubs, stamps, postcards, maps, brochures, and souvenirs you have collected during your exciting trip to Washington, D.C. Share your scrap book with all your friends and family.

Phillips
Museum
Shop & Café

Museum
Entrance on
21st Street

my trip to Washington, D.C.

WORLD WAR II MEMORIAL

This magnificent memorial honoring the 18 million who served in the armed forces of the U.S., the more than 400,000 who died, and all who supported the war effort from home, opened to the public on April 29, 2004. Fifty-six 17' granite pillars connected by a bronze sculpted rope celebrate the unity of our nation during WWII. Look at the flagpole bases to see the military service seals of the Army, Navy, Marine Corps, Army Air Forces, Coast Guard and Merchant Marine.

Day I visited

_____

The first thing I noticed was

_____

I really enjoyed

_____
_____
_____
_____
_____

I learned that

_____
_____
_____
_____
_____
_____

Seeing this memorial made me feel

_____
_____
_____

my trip to Washington, D.C.

No, this city isn't named after George Washington, but after George II, the reigning king of England when it was founded. As you wander down the picturesque cobblestone streets, remember that during the 1700s, this was a tobacco outpost which eventually grew into a major port by the end of the 18th–century. Initially it had maintained itself as a separate entity from the capital, but in 1871 when it suffered a financial crisis it merged with Washington.

Georgetown

Day I visited

_____

The first thing I noticed was

_____

The streets reminded me of

_____

_____

_____

_____

My favorite building was

_____

_____

_____

_____

_____

_____

I would/wouldn't like to come back here because

_____

_____

my trip to Washington, D.C.

67

As the sixth largest religious structure in the world, this Gothic structure has 215 stained glass windows, 200 carved angels, and 100 gargoyles. Construction began in 1907, and it wasn't finished until 1990, but it was well worth the wait. As you wander through the Cathedral, be aware that you are following in the footsteps of such famous people as Martin Luther King, Elizabeth II and other various world famous figures.

Washington National
Cathedral

Day I visited

_____

The first thing I noticed was

_____

The best part of the cathedral was

_____
_____
_____
_____
_____

When I was inside I felt

_____
_____
_____
_____
_____
_____

I would/wouldn't like to come back here because

_____
_____
_____

my trip to Washington, D.C.

US NAVAL
Observatory

The truth is out there and you can find it through the 32-foot telescope which gives you a look at stars over 25,000 light years away! Or, take a look at the moon to see what it's really made of. This facility is responsible for collecting astronomical data for the government.

Day I visited

_____

The first thing I noticed was

_____

The most amazing thing I saw was

_____
_____
_____
_____

I learned that

_____
_____
_____
_____
_____

I'm going to tell my friends

_____
_____

my trip to Washington, D.C.

Mad Lib ™

Before looking at the story below, write in what ever words come to mind-in the columns below. Then, fill in the blank spaces with the words-you have picked according to number.

1. Adjective _____
2. Noun _____
3. Adjective _____
4. Person's name _____
5. Verb _____
6. Noun _____
7. Noun _____
8. Adjective _____
9. Noun _____
10. Exclamation _____
11. Adverb _____
12. Verb ending in "ing" _____

13. Noun _____
14. Adjective _____
15. Adjective _____
16. Adjective _____
17. Verb _____
18. Plural Noun _____
19. Verb ending in "ing" _____
20. Exclamation _____
21. 1st person's name _____
22. Adverb _____
23. Adjective _____
24. Noun _____

Dear Diary,

Today my breakfast tasted pretty 1 _____. I usually eat a/an 2 _____ _____, so I felt 3 _____. Later I met up with 4 _____ _____ to 5 _____. Instead we decided to visit a/an 6 _____, so we paid for a/an 7 _____ and went down the road until we ran into a/an 8 _____ 9 _____. 10 "_____!" I said, 11 _____ as we went 12 _____ _____ across the 13 _____. "Did you see how 14. _____ that looked?" I wonder if there are any 15 _____ and 16 _____ _____ museums here?" Let's 17 _____ to the information booth to see if they list any other 18 _____. Then we can spend the rest of the day 19 _____. 20 "_____!" 21 _____ said, 22 _____. "Being friends with you is like being friends with a/an 23 _____ 24 _____.".

my trip to **Washington, D.C.**

Lions, and tigers, and bears, oh my! Home to more than 5,000 animals, you're sure to see some you've never seen before. Created by an act of Congress in 1889, these 163 acres of wildlife host a re-created Rainforest, an incredible butterfly exhibit, Asian elephants, rhinos, giraffe and more. Pay a visit the Great Flight Cage, an open aviary, where you can wander amongst free-flying birds. Be sure to check out the "Think Tank" where the orangutans are flying 45' above your head!

National Zoological Park

Day I visited

_____

The first thing I noticed was

_____

The most unusual animal I saw was

_____
_____
_____
_____
_____

I really liked the

_____
_____
_____
_____
_____
_____

I'll tell my friends about

_____
_____

my trip to Washington, D.C.

Embassy ROW

Get ready to view some magnificent mansions! These homes to the foreign embassies and chanceries (office buildings) sport some of the most lavish and meticulously maintained grounds anywhere with their rolling lawns and palatial appearance. On your tour try to see how many different countries you can list. There are around 150 different ones.

Day I visited
_____

The first embassy I saw was
_____

The most interesting embassy was
_____
_____
_____
_____

I saw embassies from
_____
_____
_____
_____
_____
_____

The nicest embassy was
_____
_____
_____

my trip to Washington, D.C.

The Phillips collection

Y ou can thank Duncan Phillips for this museum, for in 1918 he started to collect art to establish this memorial to his father and brother who died within thirteen months of each other. This absolutely astounding collection of work includes Cezanne, Degas, Monet, Sisley, and Renoir to name a few. As you gaze upon the pieces, notice the dreamlike quality that emanates from each one and reflect on what the artist might have been trying to tell you. Write a poem about what you feel as you contemplate the images before you.

Day I visited

_____

The first thing I noticed was

_____

My favorite work was

_____
_____
_____
_____

My poem

_____
_____
_____
_____
_____
_____

I would/wouldn't like to come back here because

_____
_____
_____

Washington, D.C.

The National Geographic Museum at
Explorers Hall

A group of scientists, including Alexander Graham Bell started the National Geographic Society in 1888 when they founded a small technical bulletin all about science. Today that bulletin exists as National Geographic and the Society funds the field work of explorers, anthropologists and archaeologists all around the world. Inside you'll see the fruits of all the funding and labor that the Society has generated over the years in the areas of astronomy, oceanography, geography, and more! Be sure to check out the geochron (world time map) and the 4-billion year old moon rock!

Day I visited

_____

The first thing I noticed was

_____

My favorite exhibit was

_____
_____
_____
_____

I thought the geochron was

_____
_____
_____
_____
_____
_____

I will tell my friends about

_____
_____
_____

my trip to Washington, D.C.

ARLINGTON
National Cemetery

Created in 1864 by the U.S. Government, this cemetery is now the resting place of many notables such as John F. Kennedy, his wife Jackie, and his brother Robert. Only Presidents and their family members, members of the Supreme Court, Congress, Cabinet and some military veterans can be buried here. Also found here is the Tomb of the Unknowns, where unknowns from World Wars I, II, and the Korean War are buried.

Day I visited

_____

The first thing I noticed was

_____

Visiting here made me feel

_____
_____
_____
_____

I saw the graves of

_____
_____
_____
_____
_____

I would/wouldn't like to come back here because

_____
_____
_____

my trip to Washington, D.C.

THE PENTAGON

Count the flags! This five-sided structure supposedly designed in 3 days, built in 16 months, displays many flags. All the state flags are in one corridor, NATO flags in another, and numerous displays of other flags are hanging outside many doorways. Curiously, rumor has it that this home to the Department of Defense has a single purple water fountain in one of the basement passageways, but nobody knows why. Must be "classified" information. Currently the Pentagon is closed to visitors.

Day I visited

_____

The first thing I noticed was

_____

The building reminded me of

_____
_____
_____
_____

I saw flags from

_____
_____
_____
_____
_____
_____

I will tell my friends about

_____
_____

my trip to Washington, D.C.

Considered to be the handsomest town in Virginia, this once thriving major port on the Western shore of the Potomac River was founded by Scottish tobacco merchants in 1749. Meander down the cobblestone streets and treat yourself to a view of 18th- and 19th-century maritime buildings. Visit the Ramsay House Visitors Center where you can experience a faithful reconstruction of Alexandria's very first house!

Old Town ALEXANDRIA

Day I visited

_____

The first thing I noticed was

_____

My favorite building was

_____
_____
_____
_____

I would/wouldn't like to have lived back then because

_____
_____
_____
_____
_____
_____

What I'll remember most

_____
_____
_____

my trip to Washington, D.C.

MOUNT *Vernon*

George Washington really did sleep here! In 1761 he inherited the property and over time divided the acreage into five working farms. He also transformed the frame exterior using a process called "rustication," which involves replacing the plain wooden siding with bevel-edged pine blocks that had been coated with a mixture of paint and sand to give the appearance of stone. Be sure to stand on the back porch and look at the spectacular view of the Potomac River!

Day I visited

_____

The first thing I noticed was

_____

The best part of the house was

_____
_____
_____
_____

The most interesting thing I would tell my friend is

_____
_____
_____
_____
_____
_____

I'll tell my friends about

_____
_____
_____

my trip *to* Washington, D.C.

Go tropical in this lovely exotic garden lush with banana, coffee, palm and rubber trees. Of special interest is the "Peace Tree," grafted from a fig and rubber plant to symbolize the coming together of cultures, a "cross culture" if you will, that demonstrates how even though we are different, we can become one. Ponder on this special plant as you gaze into the tropical reflecting pool, watched over by the Aztec God of Flowers.

aztec garden

Day I visited

_____

The first thing I noticed was

_____

As I looked at all the flowers I felt

_____
_____
_____
_____

My favorite part of the garden was

_____
_____
_____
_____
_____
_____

I would/wouldn't like to come back here because

_____
_____
_____

my trip to Washington, D.C.